This Little Piggy...

by R. Eugene Jackson

Baker's Plays
7611 Sunset Blvd.
Los Angeles, CA 90042
BAKERSPLAYS.COM

CHARACTERS

MOMMY (or Daddy if male)
RACHEL (or Ronnie if male), a small child

The Five Little Pigs:
    PEGGY PIG, momma pig, the most sensible
    HENRY PIG, daddy pig
    PIGTAIL, female child pig
    PIGSTY, male (or female) child pig
    OINKIE, female (or male) a pig the same age as Rachel

RALPH, a rooster
GRETCHEN, a hen
HENRIETTA, a hen
Children:
    JOANSIE, or Johnny if male
    MELISSA, or Milton if male
    BYRON, or Babs if female
DOG, male (or female)
CAT, female (or male)
Other farm animals as desired

NOTE

The names of some characters other than the pigs may be changed to reflect the gender or ethnic makeup of the cast. When the gender of any character is changed, be sure to alter all the related pronouns ("he" to "she," etc.).

Because of their large number of lines, the roles of Rachel and Oinkie should be played by actors older than five years.

This Little Piggy went to market,
This Little Piggy stayed home;
This Little Piggy had roast beef,
This Little Piggy had none;
And this Little Piggy said, "Wee, wee, wee" all the way home.

Scene One

*(At the right side of the stage [the audience's left] is
a bed. At left is a table with several chairs or benches
around it. There are two entrances right and two left.
The present.)*

*(AT RISE: The lights fade up on stage right where
MOMMY, wearing an apron, sits on the edge of the bed
and looks off right.)*

MOMMY. Come on, Rachel. Time for bed. *(pause)* Honey,
what are you doing?

*(**RACHEL** appears at the door right in her nightie or pajamas. She carries a toothbrush and has a huge mouthful
of toothpaste suds with, if possible, bubbles coming from
her mouth. Liquid soap suds applied to her mouth may
be helpful.)*

RACHEL. Brushing my teeth.

MOMMY. *(She grabs a towel and goes to her.)* Brushing your
teeth? It looks like you're giving them a bubble bath.

RACHEL. *(excited at the idea)* Oh, Mommy, may I? May I give
them a bubble bath? They'd really like that.

MOMMY. *(She wipes **RACHEL**'s mouth.)* I don't think so, honey.
You don't want to put soap in your mouth. It doesn't
taste good. And it's not good for you.

RACHEL. That's okay. I like this new toothpaste.

MOMMY. *(She takes the toothbrush, sets it aside, and leads
RACHEL to the bed.)* Did you wash your face?

RACHEL. Oh, yes.

MOMMY. And your hands?

RACHEL. Oh, Mommy.

MOMMY. And your toes?

RACHEL. My toes?!

MOMMY. Let me see. *(She puts* **RACHEL** *on the bed and examines her toes.)* Well, they look pretty clean.

RACHEL. *(She sniffs and looks offstage left.)* I smell something.

MOMMY. *(teasing her)* Really?

RACHEL. It smells like…oh, Mommy, are you baking a cake?

MOMMY. Maybe.

RACHEL. But why? Is this a special day?

MOMMY. Tomorrow. Tomorrow is a special day.

RACHEL. What's special about it?

MOMMY. Don't you know?

RACHEL. Un-unh.

MOMMY. Well, then, we'll talk about it tomorrow. How about that? Come on, now. Into bed with you. *(She tries to pull the covers over* **RACHEL.***)*

RACHEL. *(She pushes the covers aside.)* Tell me a story.

MOMMY. A bedtime story?

RACHEL. About my toes.

MOMMY. Your toes?

RACHEL. *(She giggles.)* Yes.

MOMMY. *(She thinks.)* Hmmm. Okay.

RACHEL. Okay.

MOMMY. *(She wiggles* **RACHEL***'s big toe.)* This little piggy went to market.

RACHEL. What?

MOMMY. *(She wiggles the next toe.)* This little piggy stayed home.

RACHEL. Why?

MOMMY. *(She wiggles the middle toe.)* This little piggy had roast beef.

RACHEL. Yummy.

MOMMY. *(She wiggles her fourth toe.)* This little piggy had none.

RACHEL. Poor little piggy.

MOMMY. And this little piggy cried "Wee, wee, wee" all the way home. *(She laughs and pretends to eat RACHEL's toes.)* Mmmm-mmm, good.

RACHEL. *(She giggles and pulls her toes back and looks at them.)* But, Mommy, these are my toes. Why are you calling them little piggies?

MOMMY. Well, it's a story, honey. You wanted to hear a story. That was it.

RACHEL. No. I want to hear more. Why did this little piggy go to the market? *(She points to her big toe.)* And why did this piggy stay home? *(She points to her second toe.)* I want to know. Tell me, tell me. Please, Mommy.

MOMMY. Well, okay. Then will you go to sleep?

RACHEL. Unh-hunh. *("Yes")*

MOMMY. You understand, I'm making this up.

RACHEL. Oh, good. That's the best kind.

MOMMY. Okay. Imagine, now, that your toes are little piggies.

RACHEL. Oh, Mommy, that's silly.

MOMMY. Well, it's the only way I can tell the story. Can you imagine them as pigs?

RACHEL. I'll try.

MOMMY. *(She wiggles RACHEL's big toe.)* This little Piggy went to market. Can you imagine it?

RACHEL. I'm trying.

MOMMY. Close your eyes and try real hard.

RACHEL. *(She scrunches up her face to try. Then she smiles.)* Oh, yes! Mommy I can see her. I can see the little Piggy going to the market.

(Lights fade up on the downstage area [that stage area closest to the audience] and **PEGGY,** *a mother pig, enters from down right and crosses to down left where her purse, tote bag, and shawl are hanging on a hat rack or sitting on a table. She wears an apron identical to* **MOMMY***'s.)*

PEGGY. *(as she removes her apron)* Market, market, market. Gotta go to the market. Gotta get a few things at the market.

(She picks up her purse and rifles through it as she does a few pig grunts.)

PEGGY. *(cont.)* Let's see. Do I have my wallet? *(She pulls it out.)* Yes. Cash? No. Checkbook? No. Credit cards? Ah!! Yes! Credit cards.

(She puts the wallet back into her purse and pulls out a small bottle of mouth wash.)

Mouth wash? Never can be too careful about my breath.

(She removes the cap, takes a mouthful, and gargles. Then she looks around for someplace to spit it out. She gets a panicked look on her face. She looks desperately. Finally, she spits it back into the bottle. She stares at the bottle.)

I don't think I want to use that bottle again.

(She puts the lid back on and puts it back into her purse. Then she rifles through her purse again.)

My grocery list. Did I remember to bring my grocery list?

(She pulls out a short end of a very, very long piece of paper. The paper rolls found on adding machines would work well.)

Yes, yes, yes. Grocery list.

(She pulls it out of her purse. She keeps pulling and pulling as the list grows longer and longer. She pauses.)

A long grocery list. *(She pulls more and pauses.)* A *very* long grocery list. A very, *very* long grocery list. I'll never be able to carry all this. *(She stuffs it back into her purse.)* But I'll carry as much as I can. *(She calls back toward up left.)* Henry, you'll have to stay home while I go to the market.

(She does some pig grunts and exits down left. The downstage Lights fade to black.)

RACHEL. But, Mommy, why is she going to the market?

MOMMY. Well, that's part of the story, Rachel. You'll see later. Now see if you can visualize the little Piggy that stayed home.

RACHEL. *(She tries.)* I can't. I can't see that Piggy.

MOMMY. Well, imagine that it's you. And you have to stay home.

RACHEL. But I don't want to stay home. *(pause)* Wait.

MOMMY. What do you see?

RACHEL. I see…I see the second little Piggy. But he's a big Piggy. And he's not very happy.

*(The lights fade up downstage as **HENRY**, the father pig, enters from up left with a broom, a mop and pail of water, a dusting cloth, a spray can of cleaner, and anything else he can stuff into his mouth, hands, arms, underarms, and his pockets. In other words, he is loaded down with cleaning supplies. He even carries one or more items between his legs that make him walk awkwardly.)*

HENRY. *(He grumbles.)* "Stay at home, Henry; Stay at home, Henry; Stay at home, Henry." I think I'm going to change my name to…to Gilla-ma-tilla. Or Silla-ma-trilla. Or Milla-ma-billa-trilla. Or something worse. Then when she says "Stay at home, Henry," she won't be talking to me…because I'll be Gilla-ma-tilla. *(pause)* "Clean the house, Henry; Clean the house, Henry; Clean the house, Henry." *(He looks at everything he's carrying.)* I don't think I have enough supplies.

*(**PIGTAIL** enters from up left. A young girl pig wearing a pigtail hairdo, she is eating a roast beef sandwich. If **PIGTAIL** is played by a male, his name can refer to his curly tail.)*

PIGTAIL. This roast beef is delicious, daddy.

HENRY. *(grumbling)* Great. Now I'll have to clean the kitchen again.

RACHEL. *(to **MOMMY**)* I can see the little Piggy with the roast beef.

(**PIGSTY**, *a young boy and dressed similar to* **PIGTAIL** *except that he is filthy from head to foot, enters from up left with a slice of bread in each hand.*)

PIGSTY. (*to* **HENRY**, *indicating* **PIGTAIL**) Daddy, Pigtail ate all the roast beef.

HENRY. So?

RACHEL. (*to* **MOMMY**) And there's the one with none.

PIGSTY. So I'm hungry.

PIGTAIL. Daddy, Pigsty is too dirty to eat.

PIGSTY. No, I'm not. And if she has all the roast beef, what am I supposed to put on this bread?

HENRY. Mayonnaise and mustard.

PIGSTY. That doesn't sound very tasty.

HENRY. Then add some catsup.

PIGSTY. Oh. Okay. That might be good. (*He exits up left.*)

PIGTAIL. Sounds yucky to me. (*She exits up left.*)

HENRY. (*still grumbling*) "Clean the house, Henry; Clean the house, Henry; Clean the house, Henry." (*He looks off left angrily.*) Well, first I'll have to clean little Pigsty! If I can catch him. (*He waddles off up left with all his supplies.*)

(*There is a slight pause.*)

RACHEL. But where is the little Piggy that said "Wee, wee, wee" all the way home?

(**OINKIE**, *a female, and at five years old, the youngest of the pigs, enters from up right carrying a teddy bear in one hand and crosses left.*)

OINKIE. (*Her sound is a cross between a pig grunt and an unhappy cry.*) Wee, wee, wee, wee, wee, weeeee! (*She exits up left.*)

(*The downstage lights fade to black.*)

RACHEL. What's she crying about, Mommy?

MOMMY. I'll get to that. Why don't we go back and start at the very beginning.

RACHEL. Oh, goodie!

MOMMY. Before the first Piggy went to market, and before the last little Piggy cried…

MOMMY/RACHEL. *(in unison)* "Wee, wee, wee all the way home." *(They giggle together.)*

MOMMY. Okay. So, once upon a time, there were…?

RACHEL. Five.

MOMMY. Five little piggies.

RACHEL. Like my five little toes.

MOMMY. Yes. Like your little toes. And they lived together in a big barn.

RACHEL. A barn?

MOMMY. That's where all pigs live. It's called a pig-sty.

RACHEL. Okay.

MOMMY. Outside, there's mud for the pigs to wallow in.

RACHEL. They wallow in mud?

MOMMY. To stay cool.

RACHEL. Why don't they just turn on the air conditioning?

MOMMY. Barns don't have air conditioning, Rachel.

RACHEL. Oh. Well, go on. I like this story.

MOMMY. Once upon a time, there were five little piggies… who lived in a pigsty…that looked very much like our very own home.

*(The stage lights fade to black as **MOMMY** and **RACHEL** exit unseen. Then the lights fade up on the entire stage.)*

Scene Two

*(The full interior of the house; the present. **PEGGY**'s purse, shawl, and tote bag are near the front door at down left.)*

*(**AT RISE**: **HENRY** is totally hidden under a blanket on the bed. Wearing an apron and carrying a spoon and pot, **PEGGY** enters from the up left doorway.)*

PEGGY. *(She calls loudly toward the right as she bangs on the pot with the spoon.)* Rise and shine! Rise and shine for all little piggies! Time to get up. Time to greet the day with big smiles on your faces.

*(**PIGTAIL** enters from up right as **PIGSTY** enters from down right. They rub the sleep out of their eyes and stretch and yawn and snort pig grunts.)*

PIGTAIL. What's for breakfast, momma?

PEGGY. Well, you're a pig, Pigtail. What do you think is for breakfast?

PIGTAIL. Slop?

PEGGY. That's right. Leftovers from the humans' meals.

PIGTAIL. Oh, yum-yum!

PIGSTY. Oh, no-no!

PEGGY. What is it, Pigsty? I thought you liked slop. All pigs like slop.

PIGSTY. Yeah, but Pigtail will eat it all.

PEGGY. There's plenty for everybody.

PIGSTY. Until she gets her snout into it. Then it's all gone. She eats like a…like a…like a pig!

PIGTAIL. Well, pigs are supposed to eat like pigs.

PIGSTY. But you eat like ten pigs rolled up into one.

PIGTAIL. And you haven't taken a bath in ten days.

PIGSTY. *(proudly)* Eleven days!

PEGGY. *(She turns to the bed and bangs the pot again.)* You, too, Henry. Up and at 'em.

HENRY. *(He peeks from under the blanket.)* The sun can't be coming up at this hour.

PEGGY. It's not.

HENRY. Oh, good. Then I can go back to sleep. *(He pulls the blanket back over his head.)*

PEGGY. It's been up for an hour.

HENRY. *(He looks out again.)* Oh. Well, call me when it's been up for two hours. *(He pulls it over him again.)*

PEGGY. Henry! This is a very important day.

HENRY. *(He crawls out of bed and stands.)* I know, I know.

PEGGY. And I need your help.

HENRY. *(sleepily)* I wish I could help, Peggy, but I'm still asleep.

PEGGY. But you're standing right here.

HENRY. I may be standing right here, but I'm still asleep. *(He tilts his head over and snores.)*

PEGGY. Henry, wake up! *(She bangs on the pot again.)*

HENRY. *(He awakens, snorting.)* All right, all right. I'm awake. I just *wish* I were still asleep.

PEGGY. I've made a list of chores for each of you. *(She hands each of them a list.)* After you finish these, then you can go back to sleep.

HENRY. *(Looks at his long list.)* After I finish all these, I'll be dead!

PEGGY. Henry!

HENRY. All right, all right. I'll do them. But I'll be doing them in my sleep.

PEGGY. Doesn't matter. As long as they get done.

PIGTAIL. What about our breakfast slop?

PEGGY. You can eat while you work.

PIGSTY. What about Oinkie?

PEGGY. We'll let the baby sleep a little longer. After all, we're going to surprise her.

PIGTAIL. Oh, yum-yum! I love surprises!

PIGSTY. She said the surprise is for Oinkie.

PIGTAIL. I don't care. I still love surprises.

PEGGY. Right now, it's time for your chores. Go on, now. Get to work.

PIGTAIL. Food first. *(She runs into the kitchen – the door upstage left.)*

PIGSTY. Leave some for me. *(He runs off after her.)*

HENRY. Do you think this plan will work?

PEGGY. Only if you finish your chores first.

HENRY. *(reads from his list)* "Clean the mud out back." How can I "clean the mud?" You can't clean mud. Mud is dirty. And wet. That's why it's called mud.

PEGGY. Take the shovel and smooth it out.

HENRY. Oh.

PEGGY. And get all the trash out of it. When I was wallowing yesterday, I laid on a stone, and my arm still hurts.

HENRY. Oh, all right. *(He gets a shovel leaving against a wall and holds it.)*

PEGGY. But make up the bed first.

HENRY. Whatever you say, dear. *(He puts the shovel back against the wall.)*

PIGTAIL. *(She enters with a bowl of slop and eats with her fingers. She has food all over her mouth.)* Good slop, Mom.

PEGGY. Pick up your room.

PIGTAIL. Do I have to?

PEGGY. Go!

> *(***PIGTAIL*** licks her fingers and exits up right. ***HENRY*** gets back into bed, and covers himself with the blanket. ***PIGSTY*** enters from up left eating an apple.)*

PIGSTY. I got to this apple before Pigtail did. It's good.

PEGGY. Pick up your room.

PIGSTY. I can't right now.

PEGGY. Why not?

PIGSTY. Because it takes both my hands to eat this apple.

PEGGY. Go!

PIGSTY. Ohhhh!

> *(He snorts and exits down right. **PEGGY** hears **HENRY**'s snoring and turns to him.)*

PEGGY. Henry, you're supposed to be making up the bed.

HENRY. I can't.

PEGGY. Why not?

HENRY. Because somebody's in it.

PEGGY. Who's in it?

HENRY. I am.

PEGGY. *(loudly)* Well, get out of it!

HENRY. *(She bangs loudly on the pot, and the noise rattles **HENRY** so badly he nearly falls out of the bed.)* Yes, right. I'm on it. 'Nuff said.

PEGGY. Now fluff the pillows while I check on the coffee.

> *(He snorts and sleepily fluffs one pillow as she exits up left. **PIGSTY** enters from down right carrying a toy.)*

PIGSTY. What do I do with this?

HENRY. I don't know. Ask your momma.

PIGSTY. *(He yells as he exits up left.)* Momma, what do I do with this? Momma?!

> *(**PIGTAIL** enters from up right with a doll.)*

PIGTAIL. Daddy, my doll needs a new head.

HENRY. Why?

PIGTAIL. Because she's tired of this one.

HENRY. You can't just change heads because you want to.

PIGTAIL. *(She cries.)* Waaaaa! My doll wants a new head!

PEGGY. *(enters from up left)* Henry, what did you say to make her cry?

PIGTAIL. *(She abruptly stops crying.)* Is there any slop left in the kitchen, momma?

PEGGY. There's plenty to eat, Pigtail.

PIGTAIL. Oh, yum-yum.

PEGGY. Where's the bowl you took into your room?

PIGTAIL. In my room. *(She exits up left.)*

PEGGY. *(calls after her)* You can't leave it in there. *(pause)* I guess she can leave it in there. For now. *(She turns to* **HENRY**.*)* You can fluff the other one now, Henry.

HENRY. Oh, good. I was getting tired of doing this one. *(He tosses the first pillow down and picks up the second one.)*

PEGGY. And then sweep the floor and mop.

HENRY. Remind me why we're doing all this cleaning.

PEGGY. *(She smiles.)* You know.

HENRY. *(He smiles.)* Yeah, well, okay.

> *(***PIGSTY*** *enters from up left, eating a banana and carrying the toy.)*

PEGGY. *(to* **PIGSTY***)* Into the toy box.

PIGSTY. Okay.

PEGGY. You know where your toy box is, don't you?

PIGSTY. Yeah. It's under everything else. But don't worry. I'll find it. *(He exits down right.)*

HENRY. *(as he picks up the broom and sweeps)* I hope little Oinkie is worth all this.

PEGGY. *(lightly scolding)* Henry!

HENRY. Oh, she is; she is. I'm just saying.

PEGGY. I want everything to be perfect. She'll be so excited.

> *(***PIGTAIL*** *enters from up left with her doll's head in one hand and its body in the other.)*

PIGTAIL. See? I took her head off so you can replace it easier.

HENRY. You what? *(He puts the pillow down and takes the doll in one hand and the head in the other.)*

> *(***PIGSTY*** *enters empty-handed from down right.)*

PIGSTY. All done. *(He brushes his hands off.)*

PEGGY. *(to* **PIGSTY***)* What did you do with the banana peel? And that apple you were eating?

PIGSTY. I did just what you said, Momma. I put them in the toy box.

PEGGY. No, no, no! You don't put your food in the toy box. You put your toys in the toy box.

PIGSTY. Oh.

PEGGY. No wonder your room looks like a pigsty – and smells even worse.

*(The four of them ad-lib some noisy conversation, the adults trying to correct them, and the children trying to explain. In the middle of the debate, **OINKIE** enters from up right. She carries her teddy bear in one hand.)*

OINKIE. Momma?

PEGGY. What? *(She sees **OINKIE**. To **HENRY**, **PIGTAIL**, and **PIGSTY**)* Shhhh!

*(They cut off all their conversation and turn to **OINKIE**.)*

OINKIE. You woke me up.

PEGGY. *(She goes to her.)* Oh, so sorry, baby. We didn't mean to. Are you ready for some breakfast?

OINKIE. Not that pig slop again.

PEGGY. Now, now, Oinkie, I know you love it.

OINKIE. I just thought there might be sometime else. You know, like a cake, maybe.

PEGGY. A cake for breakfast? Don't be silly. Pigtail, take care of your little sister. I've got to go to the market for a few things.

PIGSTY. I'm glad I don't have to take care of her. Sisters! Yuck! *(He snorts.)*

PEGGY. And Pigsty, you get all the food scraps out of your room and put them in the kitchen.

PIGSTY. Oh, Momma!

PEGGY. We'll have them for lunch. *(She grabs a shawl near the front door down left, puts it on, and then gets her purse and tote bag which are also near the front door.)* I'll be back soon. *(to herself)* I hope I have everything. Credit cards – yes. Shopping list – yes. *(She pulls part of the previous list from her purse and studies it.)*

PIGTAIL. I'm hungry again.

PIGSTY. Well, don't eat everything in the kitchen.

PIGTAIL. Yes, I am. *(She rushes into the kitchen.)*

PIGSTY. No, you're not. *(He chases after her.)*

OINKIE. What about me?

HENRY. Follow the herd.

OINKIE. *(as she rushes into the kitchen with her normal cry)* Wee, wee, weeee.

HENRY. Peggy?

PEGGY. *(at the door)* Yes, dear?

HENRY. *(in desperation)* Hurry back!

PEGGY. Henry?

HENRY. Yes, dear?

PEGGY. Clean the house.

HENRY. Clean the house. Right. As soon as I put this doll back together. *(He holds up the head in one hand and the body in the other.)*

*(**PEGGY** blows him a kiss and exits down left.)*

Clean the house, Henry; clean the house, Henry; clean the house, Henry. I need to change my name. Then when she says "Henry," she won't be talking to me. *(He looks around.)* Looks clean enough to me.

OINKIE. *(She enters from the kitchen still carrying her teddy bear. Trying to appear innocent.)* Uhhh, do you know what today is, daddy?

HENRY. Of course, I know what today is. It's, uh, Tuesday. Umm, Monday? I know it's one of those. Or it could be Thursday.

OINKIE. No, I meant what special day is today?

HENRY. Mondays are always special.

OINKIE. No, I meant what special, special day?

HENRY. Oinkie, why don't you go outside and play with the chickens.

OINKIE. But….

HENRY. Or the goats.

OINKIE. But….

HENRY. Or you can stay in here and help me clean the house.

OINKIE. *(slight pause)* I think I'd rather go outside.

HENRY. Good.

OINKIE. *(She starts down left and pauses at the door.)* But today is a very special day.

HENRY. Go!

OINKIE. If I have to. *(She exits sadly down left.)*

HENRY. *(to himself)* I want to tell her, but I can't. Not just yet. *(He looks up right.)* Ah, well. The bedrooms first.

(He smiles and exits up right as the lights fade out on the interior and fade up on the downstage area.)

Scene Three

(In the barnyard; immediately following.)

(AT RISE: **GRETCHEN** *and* **HENRIETTA**, *two hens, enter from down right carrying an open A-frame stepladder, and chatter loudly with some chicken "cluck-clucks" thrown in.* **RALPH**, *a rooster, follows them to supervise their activities. He is always exasperated at their constant and loud chatter.)*

GRETCHEN. *(amid the chatter)* And Mildred said she laid a dozen eggs in one sitting. Can you believe that? Twelve eggs?

HENRIETTA. *(after a few chicken noises)* No! She lies.

GRETCHEN. You can always count on her to tell big ones.

HENRIETTA. Or she forgot how to count.

GRETCHEN. More likely, she never learned.

HENRIETTA. She probably laid two eggs.

GRETCHEN. And forgot to put on her glasses. You know she can't see without her glasses.

HENRIETTA. So she sees two eggs and thinks they're twelve eggs.

GRETCHEN. So she doesn't know how many eggs she laid.

HENRIETTA. Or she laid one egg and tells us it was a dozen eggs just so she can brag about it.

GRETCHEN. She likes to brag. And, if she doesn't have anything to brag about, she makes it up.

HENRIETTA. She makes up stories all the time.

GRETCHEN. I've heard her make up lots of stories.

HENRIETTA. Does it all the time.

(They cluck loudly and get even louder.)

ROOSTER. *(at the end of his patience)* Will you two shut up about Mildred's dozen eggs!

GRETCHEN. Two eggs.

HENRIETTA. We've decided it was two eggs.

ROOSTER. I don't care if it was two eggs or twenty eggs.

GRETCHEN. Twenty eggs? Nobody can lay twenty eggs at one sitting.

HENRIETTA. Can they?

GRETCHEN. Not possible.

(They cluck loudly.)

ROOSTER. Stop it! Stop it, stop it, stop it!

GRETCHEN. Stop what?

HENRIETTA. What's he talking about?

ROOSTER. *(like a rooster)* Cock-a-doodle-doooooo!

GRETCHEN. *(as both* HENS *hold their ears)* Aeeeiiii!

HENRIETTA. Will you stop cock-a-doodle-do-ing!

GRETCHEN. It hurts our ears.

HENRIETTA. Besides, you're supposed to cock-a-doodle-doo at sunrise.

GRETCHEN. Which you forgot to do this morning.

ROOSTER. I overslept. I had a late night.

HENRIETTA. Which made us all late in getting up.

ROOSTER. What does it matter? All you do is lay a few eggs and sit on them all day long.

GRETCHEN. And now we've got to rush to get this ladder to the pigsty.

(They hear pig snorting off left. It is from OINKIE.*)*

ROOSTER. *(to the* HENS*)* Quiet. Shhhhh.

GRETCHEN. Quiet? You want us to be quiet? Us?

HENRIETTA. That's not possible.

ROOSTER. I hear something.

GRETCHEN. We're hens.

HENRIETTA. Cackling is what we do.

ROOSTER. It's Oinkie.

GRETCHEN/HENRIETTA. *(to each other)* Oinkie?! Shhhh!

HENRIETTA. We're caught. What are we going to do?

ROOSTER. Hide the ladder. Hurry. Before she sees it.

GRETCHEN. How can we hide the ladder?

ROOSTER. Fold it up. Put it behind something.

> *(With lots of hen noises, the two* **HENS** *clumsily move the ladder around and up and down, trying to get it to fold. Instead, they get caught in it and squeal loudly.)*

ROOSTER. I said, "Quiet!"

GRETCHEN. But we're....

HENRIETTA. Doing out best.

ROOSTER. Hurry. She's coming this way.

> *(They work with it as best they can, but they still can't get it to fold up. As* **OINKIE** *enters,* **GRETCHEN** *has her foot caught in the ladder and* **HENRIETTA** *tries to hide her and the ladder by standing in front of them.)*

ROOSTER. How can two hens be so clumsy?

GRETCHEN. It's easy. First you stick your foot in here. *(She indicates her stuck foot.)*

ROOSTER. Shush!

> *(***OINKIE** *enters from left still carrying her teddy bear. When she sees the* **ROOSTER**, *she rushes over to him.)*

OINKIE. Hi, Mr. Rooster Ralph.

ROOSTER. That's Ralph Rooster.

OINKIE. Okay.

ROOSTER. And this is Henrietta.

OINKIE. Hey, Mrs. Chicken Henrietta.

HENRIETTA. That's "Henrietta Hen."

OINKIE. Okay. And that's Gretchen Hen.

GRETCHEN. I'm "Gretchen Chicken."

OINKIE. Okay. I'm Oinkie.

ROOSTER. We know who you are, Oinkie. But we're kinda busy just now.

OINKIE. Oh. Well, if you're busy, I'll just leave.

ROOSTER. Fine. Good.

OINKIE. *(reluctantly)* Well, goodbye. *(She crosses to their right.)*

ROOSTER. Goodbye.

(The HENS *cackle their goodbyes and wave to him. Then they turn back to each other.)*

GRETCHEN. A dozen eggs. Can you believe that?

HENRIETTA. Can't believe that.

ROOSTER. Let's go…before Oinkie decides to start up another conversation. *(He starts to push them off right.)*

OINKIE. *(She turns back to them and smiles.)* Know what today is?

ROOSTER. Too late. *(Reluctantly, he turns back to* OINKIE.*)* Uh, sunny and bright?

OINKIE. Oh. I guess so. But I mean what important thing happens today?

ROOSTER. The sun comes up.

OINKIE. No. The sun comes up every day.

ROOSTER. Except when it's cloudy and raining.

OINKIE. No. The sun still comes up. It just stays behind the clouds where we can't see it.

ROOSTER. Really?

OINKIE. Yes. I learned that in kindergarten.

ROOSTER. I skipped kindergarten.

HENRIETTA. And look how stupid you are.

ROOSTER. *(angrily)* What?

HENRIETTA. Nothing, nothing. Just thinking out loud.

ROOSTER. Well, I'll do the thinking around here. You just take care of the stepladder.

OINKIE. The what?

ROOSTER. Oops. Uhhh, I didn't say that.

OINKIE. Didn't say what?

ROOSTER. Whatever it is you think you heard, I didn't say.

OINKIE. A stepladder? *(She circles around and looks at it. To* GRETCHEN.*)* Your foot's stuck in that ladder.

HENRIETTA. Uhhh, what foot?

GRETCHEN. Uhhh, what ladder?

OINKIE. The ladder your foot's stuck in.

GRETCHEN. Oh, that ladder.

HENRIETTA. Oh, that foot.

OINKIE. Let me help you get it out. *(She grunts as she tries.)*

GRETCHEN. No need. It's not stuck.

> *(***OINKIE*** *grunts loudly as she tugs on it.)*

> Ouch! Ohhhhh! Stop that! Stop it. It hurts, it hurts. *(It comes loose.)* Oh! See? Not stuck. I told you it wasn't stuck. *(to* **HENRIETTA***)* Ouch! That hurt. *(She rubs it.)*

OINKIE. *(to the* **ROOSTER***)* My birthday.

ROOSTER. What?

OINKIE. Today's my birthday.

ROOSTER. *(evasively)* Oh. Well, that's nice.

OINKIE. I thought maybe there would be a party.

ROOSTER. A party?

OINKIE. A birthday party. For me.

ROOSTER. Oh. Well, you know.

OINKIE. With a big birthday cake.

GRETCHEN. How old are you?

OINKIE. *(She holds up six fingers.)* Uh, this many. *(She holds up six fingers.)* Five.

ROOSTER. Five? Didn't you just hold up six fingers? *(to the* **HENS***)* That was six fingers, wasn't it?

GRETCHEN. Oinkie, don't you know how to count?

HENRIETTA. They don't teach them anything in kindergarten these days.

OINKIE. I'm five right now. *(She holds up five fingers.)* But I'll be six before the day is over. *(She holds up six fingers.)* Five… *(She holds up five fingers.)* Six. *(She holds up six fingers.)*

ROOSTER. Oh. Well, that makes sense. I guess.

OINKIE. And I want lots and lots of candles on the cake.

GRETCHEN. You don't get lots and lots of candles.

HENRIETTA. You only get six.

OINKIE. Well, I could pretend I'm twelve and get twelve candles.

HENRIETTA. Doesn't work that way.

OINKIE. Okay, six. Six candles. And ice cream and presents and games and songs and…and…. Well, I thought there might be a party.

ROOSTER. *(He looks around.)* I don't see any parties.

OINKIE. *(She looks around.)* I don't see any either.

ROOSTER. Well, we've got to deliver this ladder to…I mean, we need to go.

OINKIE. What are you going to do with the ladder?

GRETCHEN. *(to* **ROOSTER***)* Big mouth.

HENRIETTA. *(to* **ROOSTER***)* Now look what you've done.

ROOSTER. *(to* **OINKIE***)* Well, we're uh….

OINKIE. Yes?

GRETCHEN. Yes?

HENRIETTA. Yes? We're waiting.

ROOSTER. Well, we're going to climb up to the moon.

OINKIE/GRETCHEN/HENRIETTA. The moon?!

ROOSTER. Uhhh, yes. The moon. It's pretty high up in the sky, you know. So we need a ladder to get to it.

OINKIE. But it's daylight. The moon's not up there.

ROOSTER. Well, we'll wait until nighttime. Then we'll set up the ladder and…

GRETCHEN. And what?

ROOSTER. And the hens will climb up there…

GRETCHEN/HENRIETTA. Us?

ROOSTER. And…and bring it down so we can get a good look at it.

OINKIE. Really? You're going to bring the moon down here? To the farm? So we can look at it up close?

ROOSTER. *(proudly)* Yes! Real close.

(*The* **HENS** *begin to chatter away, telling him that's not possible and adding lots of chicken noises.*)

ROOSTER. *(He places one hand [wing] over each* **HEN***'s beak.)* Quiet!

(They try to talk with their mouths closed, but only muf-fled sounds come out.)

ROOSTER. *(to **OINKIE**)* We have to leave now. So long.

*(He looks at the **HENS** and warns them by shaking his head at them)*

Quiet. No more chatter. Understand?

*(The **HENS** nod. He releases their beaks.)*

OINKIE. I want to see it when you bring it down.

ROOSTER. Oh. Well, you can't do that.

OINKIE. Why not?

ROOSTER. Well, uhhh, we have to put it back, you know.

OINKIE. You do?

ROOSTER. Yes. Right away.

OINKIE. Why?

GRETCHEN. *(to the **ROOSTER**)* You're getting in deeper and deeper.

HENRIETTA. Answer her. Why do we have to put it back?

ROOSTER. Well, uhhh, if there were no moon in the sky, nighttime would be so dark, we couldn't see. See? It's like, you know, a big light bulb up there.

OINKIE. Oh. Like the sun is a big light bulb in the daytime.

GRETCHEN. Only brighter.

HENRIETTA. And hotter.

ROOSTER. *(to **OINKIE**)* Do you understand all that?

OINKIE. Sure.

ROOSTER. Well, I wish I did.

OINKIE. If there were no moon at night or no sun in the daytime, I couldn't see well enough to find my birth-day party.

ROOSTER. Right!

OINKIE. Only I don't see my birthday party anyway. *(sadly)* Do you?

ROOSTER. *(He looks around.)* Uh, no.

(The **HENS** *gesture to the ladder and point off right.)*

ROOSTER. Oh, yeah. We have to go now. See you later, Oinkie.

GRETCHEN. *(as she and* **HENRIETTA** *pick up the ladder)* Gotta go.

HENRIETTA. See you later.

(They cross right.)

OINKIE. *(calling after them)* If you see any birthday parties today, let me know. It might be mine. Well, bye, I guess. *(She exits left with her head lowered.)*

GRETCHEN. *(to the* **ROOSTER** *as they put the ladder on the ground)* She looks so sad.

HENRIETTA. Maybe we should tell her what we're really doing with this ladder.

ROOSTER. We can't do that. We were sworn to secrecy. Let's go.

(They chatter and, leaving the ladder behind, exit right.)

ROOSTER. *(after a brief pause, offstage)* The ladder!!!

(Clucking loudly, the **HENS** *re-enter and grab the ladder as the* **ROOSTER** *looks on. The* **HENS** *swing the ladder in various directions, almost hitting the* **ROOSTER** *and again getting entangled in it. They more or less limp off right, still squawking.)*

ROOSTER. *(to override their chatter)* Cock-a-doodle-doooo! *(They are gone.)*

(Three farm **CHILDREN** *enter from left, each carrying a big bag over his/her shoulder.)*

JOANSIE. Is that our rooster crowing?

MELISSA. Who else?

JOANSIE. He's supposed to crow at sunrise. Instead, he sleeps in – and crows at noon.

BYRON. Stupid rooster.

JOANSIE. We need to get him an alarm clock so he'll wake up in time to crow properly.

MELISSA. Yeah. He's supposed to wake us up early so we can get a good start on our daily chores.

BYRON. Stupid rooster.

JOANSIE. I just hope we have time to fix everything.

MELISSA. Someone's going to be awfully disappointed if we don't.

BYRON. You know what?

JOANSIE/MELISSA. What?

BYRON. That rooster is stupid.

JOANSIE. Okay. We get the message. Did we get everything? Melissa?

MELISSA. *(indicating her bag)* I brought the corn off the cob.

JOANSIE. That's corn *on* the cob.

MELISSA. It's on the cob now but, after we eat it, it will be corn *off* the cob.

JOANSIE. Okay. Byron, what are you bringing?

BYRON. Beans. I've got enough beans in this bag to feed every animal on the farm.

JOANSIE. Okay. Well…

BYRON. And all the farms surrounding us.

JOANSIE. Okay. Well…

BYRON. And all the farms surrounding them.

JOANSIE. Okay, okay. You've got the beans.

BYRON. I've got the beans.

MELISSA. What about you, Joansie?

JOANSIE. No, I don't have any beans.

MELISSA. I mean, what's in your bag?

JOANSIE. Flour. My bag's full of flour. So we can make bread and pastries.

BYRON. And cake!

JOANSIE. And cake. Yes.

BYRON. Lots of cakes.

JOANSIE. Lots of cakes. Yes.

BYRON. Lots and lots of cakes.

JOANSIE. Okay, okay. That's enough.

BYRON. There's never enough cake.

JOANSIE. We have enough! Now, we need to get all this food to the barn so we can....

OINKIE. *(Off left, she is crying with pig sounds.)* Wee-wee-wee-weeeee.

MELISSA. What's that?

BYRON. Sounds like a pig.

JOANSIE. Someone's crying.

BYRON. Sounds like a pig.

MELISSA. I think it's Oinkie.

BYRON. It *is* a pig.

JOANSIE. Quick – hide your bags!

MELISSA. I'll stand in front of mine and cover it up. *(She does.)*

BYRON. I'll stand behind mine and cover myself up. *(He does.)*

JOANSIE. No, Byron. Hide the bag, not yourself.

BYRON. Oh. *(as he stands in front of his bag)* What about you?

JOANSIE. Too late.

(**OINKIE** *enters from left rubbing her eyes as the* **CHIL-DREN** *try to look innocent.)*

JOANSIE. Hi, Oinkie. What's wrong? Why are you crying?

OINKIE. I'm not...I'm not crying.

JOANSIE. I see tears.

OINKIE. Those aren't tears. They're rain drops.

JOANSIE. But it's not raining.

OINKIE. Oh. Well, they're left over from the last rain.

JOANSIE. That was a month ago.

OINKIE. Well, I kept them safe – in the refrigerator. Today I took them out so I could, uh, play with them.

BYRON. I think she was crying.

MELISSA. Well, if you'll excuse us, Oinkie. We were on our way to the....

JOANSIE. *(interrupting her)* To our house. We were on our way to our house.

MELISSA. Oh, yeah. Right. To our house.

BYRON. I don't think you can keep tears in the refrigerator.

OINKIE. What's in the bags?

JOANSIE. What bags?

OINKIE. The one you're carrying, and the two they're trying to hide.

JOANSIE. Ohhhh.

OINKIE. Well?

JOANSIE. Well. Ummm, I'm carrying flour, Melissa's got corn, and Byron's bag is full of beans.

OINKIE. *(delighted)* Oh, wow! Beans and corn. I love beans and corn.

JOANSIE. And flour.

OINKIE. I don't love flour. It tastes like soft sand.

JOANSIE. Well, you don't eat it raw. You make it into things.

OINKIE. Oh. Well, then, I'm sure I'd love it.

MELISSA. How do you know?

OINKIE. I'm a pig, and pigs love anything we can eat.

BYRON. I think she was crying real tears. That's what I think.

JOANSIE. Well, we can't eat it just now.

OINKIE. Why not? I'm hungry.

JOANSIE. Well, we're on a mission.

OINKIE. What kind of mission?

MELISSA. A secret mission.

OINKIE. Tell me about it.

MELISSA. Then it wouldn't be a secret.

OINKIE. Well, okay. *(sadly)* I have a secret too. Only I didn't know it would be a secret. I thought everybody would know.

JOANSIE. Know what?

OINKIE. That today's my birthday. *(with a smile and energy)* It really is! My birthday.

(The **CHIDREN** *look back and forth at each other.)*

JOANSIE. *(without enthusiasm)* Okay. *(suddenly)* Well, we must be on our way. Come on, Melissa, Byron.

MELISSA. Coming. *(She picks up her bag.)*

BYRON. The next time I cry, I'm going to put my tears in the refrigerator.

JOANSIE. Why?

BYRON. So I can use them the next time I'm unhappy.

JOANSIE. *(pause)* Let's go. *(They pick up their bags.)*

OINKIE. I'll be six years old later today. It's the first time I've been six. And I'll probably never be six again.

JOANSIE. *(to the* **CHILDREN** *as she tries to get around* **OINKIE***)* Come on.

OINKIE. *(blocking her way)* Have you ever been six years old?

JOANSIE. Sorry, Oinkie, but we're late. *(She tries again to get around* **OINKIE.***)*

BYRON. It was the stupid Rooster that made us late. He forgot to crow this morning.

OINKIE. *(blocking her way)* It wasn't very exciting to be five. I think it'll be more exciting to be six. So I thought I would celebrate.

JOANSIE. Well, sure.

OINKIE. But I need somebody to celebrate with. I mean, somebody has to sing "Happy Birthday" to me.

MELISSA. I'm sure you'll find somebody to do that. But we're late.

BYRON. Because of that stupid Rooster.

JOANSIE. See you later, Oinkie.

(The **CHILDREN** *move to stage left and pause.* **OINKIE** *watches them, and then turns right and cries.)*

OINKIE. Wee-wee-wee-weeeeee.

MELISSA. *(to* JOANSIE*)* Do you think we should tell her, Joansie?

JOANSIE. We can't. We promised.

MELISSA. But she looks so sad.

BYRON. And she's crying. (*He moves center stage.*)

JOANSIE. Where are you going?

BYRON. To get a tear. (*He rushes to* **OINKIE** *and gently takes a tear from her face.*) Can I borrow one of these, Oinkie?

(**OINKIE** *pauses as* **BYRON** *takes a tear on his finger tip. Then* **BYRON** *rushes back to the other* **CHILDREN**.)

BYRON. I got one, I got one. I'm going to put it in my refrigerator and see how long it will last. (*He stumbles and it drops off his finger.*) Oops. It didn't last very long. Where did it go?

JOANSIE. Byron, you can come back and look for it later. Right now, we have to get to the barn.

BYRON. It was that stupid Rooster that made us late.

(*As they turn to exit left,* **OINKIE** *cries out to them.*)

OINKIE. (*in a choked voice*) If you see a birthday party any- where, let me know. It could be mine.

JOANSIE. Sure. We will. (*to the* **CHILDREN**) Let's go. (*They exit left.*)

OINKIE. Nobody knows about my birthday, and nobody cares. (*She cries as she exits right.*) Wee-wee-wee-weeee.

(*A* **DOG** *enters from left carrying an armload of decoration materials, including a two or three inch wide roll of crepe paper. Part of it is unwound and trails the* **DOG**. *A meowing and snarling* **CAT** *enters behind the* **DOG** *clawing for the paper as the* **DOG** *tries to keep it from her. The* **DOG** *runs in a circle as the* **CAT** *follows. Finally, the* **DOG** *stops and pulls the paper to himself.*)

DOG. Leave the paper alone!

CAT. (*She snarls at him and shows her claws.*) Hssstt!

DOG. (*Trying to outdo her, he growls at her.*) Grrrr!

CAT. (*She snarls bigger and claws toward him.*) Hssstt, hssstt!

DOG. (*He growls louder back at her.*) GRRRR!

CAT. I want the paper!

DOG. You can't have it!

CAT. *(She snarls her biggest snarl.)* HSSSTTT!

DOG. Yikes! You can have it. *(pause)* If you can catch it.

> *(He leaps up and down and takes off running again, this time offstage right. The* **CAT** *leaps after him. After a brief pause, the* **DOG** *re-enters from right and runs toward the left with the* **CAT** *in hot pursuit. They exit left. After another brief pause, the tired and panting* **DOG** *re-enters from left and stops at center. The tired* **CAT** *follows and stops short of the* **DOG.***)*

DOG. *(panting for breath)* I don't understand it. We both picked out this paper in the shop. But when I accidentally unrolled part of it, you started chasing it.

CAT. *(also panting for breath)* What do you think I am? I'm a cat. And you're a dumb dog. This is what cats do. We chase string and yarn and strips of paper.

DOG. But why?

CAT. Why? Because it's fun, it's fascinating, it's adventurous.

DOG. It's also witless.

CAT. Witless? What does that mean?

DOG. It means you don't have any sense.

CAT. Let me see. Dogs do stupid tricks for humans, dogs wear leashes, and dogs bury bones. So who's the dumb one here?

DOG. But I don't chase strips of paper.

CAT. You should. It's good exercise.

DOG. Okay, look. I have an idea.

CAT. I hope it's not as dumb as your other ideas.

DOG. *(He rolls the paper into a tight roll.)* See? A great big wad, but no strips. So there's nothing to chase.

CAT. Nothing to chase? Are you trying to deprive me of a little fun?

DOG. Uh, no. Not at all.

CAT. And what if it comes unrolled again?

DOG. Can't happen.

CAT. *(She snarls and claws at the paper causing it to unroll.)* It happened! *(She hisses.)* Hssstt!

DOG. Not again! Yikes!

(Trailing part of the roll of paper behind him, he runs in a few circles. The snarling **CAT** *chases it again. Suddenly the* **DOG** *stops and rips the trailing paper off the roll.)*

DOG. There. Take it. It's yours. *(He throws it at the* **CAT.** *)*

CAT. *(She lets it fall to the ground.)* Now look what you did.

DOG. What did I did?

CAT. You let it fall to the ground.

DOG. I did not let it fall to the ground.

CAT. You did!

DOG. I didn't. I *threw* it to the ground.

CAT. You know I can't chase anything that's not moving.

DOG. Oh, good. Then I'm putting all these decorations on the ground. *(He does.)*

(The **CAT** *stares at it and then at the* **DOG** *and then back at the paper.)*

CAT. Now what fun is that?

DOG. I don't like being chased.

CAT. I wasn't chasing you. I was chasing the strip of paper.

DOG. You're witless.

CAT. You're dumb.

OINKIE. *(off right)* Oink, oink. Wee-wee-weeee.

DOG. *(He looks off right.)* What's that?

CAT. *(She looks off right.)* It's Oinkie!

DOG. Oinkie? What if she sees us and all the…all the…stuff? *(He indicates the decorations on the ground.)*

CAT. *(as she runs in a hectic circle)* Hide it, hide it. We're got to hide it.

DOG. Where?

CAT. I don't know. Anywhere. Help me.

*(With lots of hissing and growling and exclamations, the two of them clumsily pick up the decorations and turn in circles to see where they can hide them. As they twist and run into each other, some of the crepe paper and other items become unwound. They flail their arms, making things worse, causing them to become so entwined in the paper and paper lanterns or whatever other decorations they have that they can hardly move. The more things that are wrapped around them, the better. They should somewhat resemble a gift-wrapped box. **OINKIE** enters from right.)*

OINKIE. *(She keeps her head down and rubs her eyes as she passes the* **CAT** *and* **DOG***.)* Hello, Cat. Hi, Dog.

DOG. *(friendly)* Hi, Oinkie. You can pet me if you want to. Or rub my belly.

CAT. *(snooty, to* **OINKIE***)* Don't talk to me. I haven't had my morning coffee yet.

OINKIE. Okay. *(He exits left.)*

DOG. *(surprised)* She hardly noticed us. *(hurt)* And she didn't rub my belly.

CAT. Fortunately, he didn't see all this...stuff...that's wrapped all around us.

DOG. Yeah. If she had, she might have become suspicious.

CAT. The cat would have been out of the bag.

DOG. What? You were in a bag?

CAT. No, I wasn't in a bag. It's an old saying–meaning the surprise would no longer be a surprise.

DOG. Okay. Well, let's get out of this mess.

CAT. Yes. I don't like being this close to a...a filthy, mangy dog.

DOG. I'm not mangy.

CAT. No. You're just filthy.

DOG. *(He smiles.)* Dogs like to get a little dirty once in a while. It's fun. And it keeps us cool.

CAT. Cats like to be clean. And we don't like to rub against dirty dogs.

DOG. Let's just get out of this.

(*As they start to unwind themselves,* **OINKIE** *re-enters from left.*)

OINKIE. (*grandly*) WHAT IS THAT?!

DOG. (*They stop.*) What is what?

CAT. I think she's pointing at us.

OINKIE. You. You look like a birthday present that somebody wrapped with his eyes closed.

DOG. Is that good or bad?

CAT. Bad.

OINKIE. I mean, you two make the ugliest gift box I've ever seen.

(*The* **DOG** *and* **CAT** *look down at themselves.*)

CAT. (*to the* **DOG**) She must be referring to you.

DOG. (*to* **OINKIE**) Yeah, well, we sorta got…uh, tied up here.

OINKIE. Well, I'll untie you. (*She crosses to them and stares at the wrappings.*) Who did this anyway?

DOG. (*pointing to the* **CAT**) She did.

CAT. (*at the same time, pointing to the* **DOG**) He did.

OINKIE. I don't know where to start. I know. I'll just rip it off. (*She starts to.*)

DOG/CAT. No!

OINKIE. (*She jumps back.*) What?

DOG. Well, I mean, don't rip it. It might hurt us.

CAT. Actually, Oinkie, we want to preserve our…wrappings as best we can.

OINKIE. Oh. Okay. (*She starts to gently unwrap them.*) But why? Why would you want to save this ugly stuff?

CAT. Ugly stuff?

OINKIE. Well, it's not very pretty.

DOG. (*to* **CAT**) She called our ugly stuff…ugly. I mean, our pretty stuff.

CAT. (*as they break out of the wrappings*) Well, look, Oinkie, if we save it, Dog and I can do this again.

DOG. Again?

CAT. Some day. Maybe. If we decide to be crazy.

DOG. I'd rather toss this ugly stuff.

CAT. *(She elbows* **DOG.** *)* We can't toss it, Dog. We need it. You know, for…you know.

DOG. Ohhh, yeah. We need it, Oinkie, for…you know.

OINKIE. No, I don't know.

DOG. *(to* **CAT** *)* She doesn't know. *(pause)* And neither do I.

CAT. *(She gives a secret wink to the* **DOG.** *)* You know. Later today.

DOG. When?

CAT. Later! Now stop asking questions.

DOG. Okay. *(pause)* Later when?

CAT. *(to* **OINKIE** *)* You can pet a dog – if you have to. But don't try to talk to them. They're just dumb animals.

DOG. Does that include me?

CAT. Oh, yeah!

OINKIE. Well, I'm just walking around. Talking to the other animals. Trying to see if any of them know what today is.

DOG. What difference does it make? I still get fed at six o'clock. *(He looks at the two of them.)* Don't I?

CAT. Today is Monday the 6th, and the time is approximately…*(She looks at the sun.)* …eleven a.m.

OINKIE. No, Cat. I mean, what is special about today?

DOG. Don't I?

CAT. Well, it's sunny. There's a pleasant breeze. A few clouds.

OINKIE. *(She whines.)* Oh, you don't know either. Why doesn't anybody know? I thought—you know, I thought maybe there would be a celebration. A party. With decorations and everything.

DOG. Decorations?

OINKIE. *(She points to their decorations.)* Oh, not those ugly things. Something nice.

DOG. *(quietly to* **CAT***)* She doesn't like our decorations.

CAT. *(trying to change the subject)* Well, Dog, I think it's time we gathered up our…lovely…decorations and went on our way.

DOG. Oh, no, you don't, Cat. If I pick up any of this stuff, you'll start a hissy fit.

CAT. No, I won't.

DOG. Well, okay.

> *(The* **DOG** *picks up a strip of paper. The* **CAT** *hisses and claws at it. The* **DOG** *throws the paper down.)*

DOG. See? See? Hissy fit!

OINKIE. Don't you want to know more about the celebration?

DOG. Sure.

CAT. *(elbowing the* **DOG***)* But not right now. We're late.

OINKIE. But I need to talk to somebody.

CAT. Sorry, Oinkie. We can't stay here any longer. Got to go. Got things to do.

> *(The* **CAT** *and* **DOG** *pick up all their stuff. The* **DOG***'s armload includes a strip of crepe paper that hangs loose.)*

DOG. Yep. Gotta go, gotta go.

OINKIE. Why?

DOG. *(He stops.)* I don't know.

CAT. Because I said so.

DOG. *(He starts moving again.)* Because Cat says so.

> *(The* **CAT** *sees the loose strip of paper, so she snarls and claws at it.)*

CAT. Hssst!

DOG. Don't do that. It scares me.

CAT. Hssssssssssssst!

DOG. That scares me even more! Yikes!

> *(The* **DOG** *runs in a circle with the* **CAT** *in hot pursuit of the strip of paper.)*

OINKIE. But what about me? Won't you talk to me? Please?

DOG. Later. Right now I've got to save myself from this ferocious Cat! *(He runs off right.)* Yikes!

CAT. And I've got to catch that strip of paper. *(She runs off after the* **DOG.***)*

OINKIE. Nobody will talk to me today.

DOG. *(He runs back on and circles* **OINKIE.***)* But you can pet me after dinner. I'll be in my doghouse.

OINKIE. Okay. I'd like that.

CAT. *(She enters still chasing the* **DOG.***)* Don't listen to Dog. He doesn't know what he's saying.

(The **DOG** *and* **CAT** *make another circle around the stage.)*

OINKIE. But if you hear anything about a birthday party today, let me know. It might be mine.

DOG. Arf, arf, arf. Sure, Oinkie. Yikes! *(He races off right howling.)* Owwwwww!

CAT. Dogs are such 'fraidy cats! *(She snarls and claws while chasing* **DOG** *off right.)*

OINKIE. And I'm such a lonely pig. I may as well go wallow in some mud. *(She cries as she exits left.)* Wee-wee-weeeeeee.

(The lights fade out.)

Scene Four

*(The interior of the **PIGS**' house; about an hour later.)*

*(**AT RISE**: As the lights fade up, **HENRY** is wearing a frilly apron and finishing up mopping the floor.)*

HENRY. *(as he leans on the mop)* Ahhh, at long last. Mopping completed!

PIGTAIL. *(She enters from up left with a sandwich in her hands.)* Daddy, Pigsty spilled something in the kitchen.

HENRY. *(to himself)* I should have known. *(to **PIGTAIL**)* What did he spill this time, Pigtail?

PIGTAIL. Everything on the kitchen table.

HENRY. *(trying to control his temper)* And what was on the kitchen table?

PIGTAIL. Lunch.

HENRY. Lunch?

PIGTAIL. Well, there was meat, potatoes, onions, peas, mayonnaise, mustard, milk, strawberry yogurt....

HENRY. *(He interrupts her.)* That settles it. I am not cleaning up another one of his messes. No. I am not. I refuse.

PEGGY. *(She enters from up left wearing her apron.)* Henry, I need you in here to clean up Pigsty's mess.

HENRY. Coming, dear. *(He exits up left.)*

PIGTAIL. *(holding up her sandwich)* I'm glad I saved my roast beef.

PIGSTY. *(enters from up left)* Momma, Pigtail took all the roast beef again. What am I supposed to eat?

PIGTAIL. If you weren't so clumsy, you could have had anything on the table.

PIGSTY. *(He holds up a bottle of catsup.)* I saved the catsup.

PEGGY. Then that's what you can eat.

PIGSTY. Oh, goodie! I love catsup. *(He uncaps the bottle and drinks from it as he exits up left.)*

PEGGY. Well, at least he didn't drop the cake. It's still in the oven.

*(There is a big racket off down left. It is the **ROOSTER** and two **HENS** manhandling the ladder. **PEGGY** and **PIGTAIL** turn their attention in that direction.)*

GRETCHEN. *(Offstage)* Turn it that way, that way.

HENRIETTA. *(Offstage)* This way?

(The ladder makes a loud noise as it is banged against something.)

GRETCHEN. No, Henrietta. That way.

HENRIETTA. Oh, I see. This way.

(The ladder is again banged against something.)

GRETCHEN. No, Henrietta, no. Let me have that thing. I'll show you.

HENRIETTA. I can do it. Let go. Let go!

GRETCHEN. Let me have it.

HENRIETTA. No!

(They cackle loudly in argument until there is a loud crash. Then silence.)

ROOSTER. *(after a pause)* I'll take the ladder.

PIGTAIL. *(Runs to the door and opens it. If there is no door, she simply runs to the opening.)* What's happening out there?

PEGGY. Who knows?

ROOSTER. *(He tries to enter, but has the ladder in a horizontal position so it bangs against the door frame.)* Ouch! *(He tries again with the same result.)* Ouch!

PIGTAIL. I'll help. *(She stands the ladder erect so it moves easily through the doorway.)* There.

ROOSTER. *(He crows.)* Cock-a-doodle-dooooo!

*(**PIGTAIL** and **PEGGY** cover their ears)*

The ladder has arrived.

GRETCHEN. *(As she enters a total mess. Her feathers are greatly ruffled, and she wears a giant bandage somewhere visible.)* And so have I.

PEGGY. Gretchen! What happened to you?

GRETCHEN. Henrietta is what happened to me.

HENRIETTA. *(She enters. She is in an equal mess with one wing in a sling.)* No. Gretchen is what happened to *me.*

ROOSTER. Actually, the ladder is what happened to them. *(He accidentally releases the ladder and it falls over him, pinning his wings to his side.)* Actually, it's what happened to all of us.

GRETCHEN. We've never handled a ladder before.

HENRIETTA. And when you have wings in place of arms, it's very complicated.

PEGGY. I'm sure. But it's very late. Please go ahead and hang the decorations.

ROOSTER. What decorations?

(The **DOG** *enters from down left carrying a bag of decorations and trailing a long piece of the crepe paper.)*

DOG. *These* decorations. *(He runs in a circle in the room.)*

CAT. *(chasing the strip of paper and snarling)* Hsssstt! Rrrar-roowww!

PEGGY. Dog, Cat, what are you doing?

DOG. I'm running from the Cat.

CAT. I'm running after the Dog.

PEGGY. Well, please stop running in the house!

PIGTAIL. Yeah, or momma will spank you.

DOG. *(He tosses the strip of paper to* **HENRIETTA.** *)* Here. You take it.

CAT. *(With a snarl, she leaps for the paper, lands on* **HENRIETTA,** *and they both fall down.)* Rrrarroowww! *(She gets the paper in her mouth.)*

HENRIETTA. *(She screams.)* Yeeeoooow!

ROOSTER. Here, Henrietta. I'll help you.

(He turns to help **HENRIETTA** *just as* **CAT** *stands. He hits* **CAT** *with the ladder, knocking her down again.)*

CAT. Rrrarroowww! *(She stands and arches her back as if to attack* **ROOSTER.** *)*

PEGGY. Stop it, stop it, stop it! Everybody take a time out. Time out. Count to ten. Go on–count.

DOG/CAT/HENS/ROOSTER/PIGTAIL. *(angrily)* One, two, three, four....

PEGGY. Not you, Pigtail.

PIGTAIL. Oh, Momma! *(She exits into the kitchen.)*

DOG/CAT/HENS/ROOSTER. *(their anger subsiding)* ...five, six, seven, eight-nine-ten. *(The last three words are spoken quickly. Then the* **ANIMALS** *relax.)*

PEGGY. I'm almost finished with things in the kitchen. Hang decorations. *(She moves to the door up left and pauses.)* No more fighting and no more crowing.

ROOSTER. But I like to crow.

PEGGY. Then you should have crowed at dawn this morning, but you slept through it.

ROOSTER. Well, I also like to sleep.

PEGGY. Decorations. Hang them. Now. *(She exits up left.)*

(If other **FARM ANIMALS** *are used, they enter from down left. If they are not used, skip the next four lines.)*

FIRST ANIMAL. Here. We'll help.

SECOND ANIMAL. I'm good at decorating things.

THIRD ANIMAL. Me, too. Give me something.

FOURTH ANIMAL. I'll take that.

(The other **ANIMALS** *make a small noise as they help the* **ROOSTER** *extricate himself from the ladder and, with the* **ROOSTER** *and* **HENS,** *some set up the ladder and hang some high decorations, while others and* **DOG** *and* **CAT** *hand them supplies and hang things at levels they can reach. Decorations include items for the table at left center. Their noises then subside so the other dialogue can be heard. If other* **ANIMALS** *are not used, the* **ROOSTER,** **HENS, DOG,** *and* **CAT** *do all the decorations. Meanwhile,* **JOANSIE, MELISSA,** *and* **BYRON** *enter carrying bowls or plates of food that they place on the table.)*

JOANSIE. *(as she shows her plate)* Here's the bread made from my flour. With the help of milk from the cows.

MELISSA. And a dozen eggs from Mildred.

GRETCHEN. A dozen eggs? You mean she actually did lay a dozen eggs in one sitting?

HENRIETTA. Amazing!

JOANSIE. And Momma Pig made a big, beautiful cake with my flour, too. *(She places her plate on the table.)*

MELISSA. And here's my corn-off-the-cob. *(pause)* Well, the corn is *on* the cob right now. *(She places her plate on the table.)*

HENRIETTA. But not for long. Corn is my favorite food.

*(There is a pause. **JOANSIE** and **MELISSA** stare at **BYRON** who is watching **ROOSTER** hang things.)*

JOANSIE/MELISSA. Byron!

BYRON. *(startled)* What?!

JOANSIE. What are you doing?

BYRON. Watching that stupid Rooster with his stupid decorations.

MELISSA. What did you bring for the party?

BYRON. What party? Oh – this party? What did I bring? Well, let's see. *(He looks into the bowl in his left hand.)* Lima beans. *(He puts that bowl on the table and looks into the bowl in his right hand.)* Pinto beans. *(He puts it on the table and looks again at his left hand.)* And…Hey, where's my third bowl?

PIGTAIL. *(She enters from the kitchen with an empty bowl.)* Here it is, Byron.

BYRON. *(He takes it and looks into it.)* It's empty! What happened to my black-eyed peas?

PIGSTY. *(enters from the kitchen)* Pigtail ate them.

PIGTAIL. I was hungry.

BYRON. You ate all of them?

PIGTAIL. I was *very* hungry.

ROOSTER. *(making an announcement)* The decorations are finished.

CAT. *(She sees a string or piece of paper hanging loose and claws at it.)* Hsstt! *(She pulls it down and struggles with it.)*

ROOSTER. Well, they *were* finished.

DOG. They'll never be finished if we don't hog-tie the Cat.

PEGGY. *(She enters from the kitchen, wiping her hands on her apron.)* There will be no "hog-tying" in my home. And no pig-tying.

DOG. How about cat-tying?

PEGGY. No tying.

HENRY. *(He enters from the kitchen with his mop.)* Well, I think I got it all cleaned up.

PIGSTY. *(He heads for the kitchen.)* I need a drink of water.

HENRY. *(bars his way)* You, Pigsty, are barred from the kitchen. Barred, banned, exiled. I don't want to have to clean up after you again.

PIGSTY. Oh, daddy!

PEGGY. *(as she looks around)* Well, everybody did a wonderful job. Oinkie will be so excited when she sees this.

HENRY. And surprised. Since we didn't tell her about it. *(He takes off his apron and puts it and the mop away.)*

PIGTAIL. A surprise birthday party!

PIGSTY. Nobody ever gave me a surprise party.

PEGGY. What about your last birthday?

PIGSTY. Well, I mean, other than that.

PEGGY. *(to the group)* So all we need now is little Oinkie.

(Everyone faces the door down left.)

HENRY. She should be here at any time now. Are we ready?

OTHERS. *(ad-libbed)* Yes!

HENRY. Okay. *(as if presenting her)* Oinkie! *(He gestures toward down left.)*

PIGTAIL. *(after a pause)* Where is she?

PIGSTY. I don't know.

HENRY. I hope she's not lost.

PEGGY. Oinkie knows her way around the farm. She's fine.

*(The lights fade down but not out on this scene and the **CHARACTERS**, still facing the down left doorway, remain still.)*

Scene Five

(Somewhere on the farm; at the same time.)

*(**AT RISE:** The lights fade up in another area, illuminating a forlorn* **OINKIE** *who is covered in mud and looks disheveled.)*

OINKIE. *(gasping for breath)* Well, I went down to the creek and wallowed in the mud. I was feeling pretty good – until that snake chased me away. A snapping turtle tried to cheer me up. But then it bit me on the... *(She points to her backside.)* ...and I felt worse. The blackberries I found made me feel better – until I fell into the bushes and got thorns stuck in me. *(She pulls a few out of her skin.)* Ouch. Ouch. Oowww – tch! And all because everybody forgot my birthday. I think I'll just stay out here in the woods and get lost. Then they'll be sorry. *(She thinks.)* Wait a minute. If I get lost, I'll be the one who's sorry. *(She looks skyward.)* Besides, it's lunch time, and I'm hungry as a pig. And pigs are always hungry. Especially at lunch time. Food. I need food. Lots and lots of food. Wallowing and running and falling have made me really, really hungry. I hope momma made a big lunch. Oh, wee, wee, wee, all the way home! *(She runs off.)*

(The lights fade out on her.)

Scene Six

(Back inside the Pigs' house; a few minutes later.)

(AT RISE: The lights fade up on the interior of the house. Everyone is still facing the door down left. Wondering where **OINKIE** *is, everyone starts talking – cackling, barking, hissing, oinking, snorting, etc.)*

ROOSTER. *(Adding his voice, he crows, as always, off-pitch.)* Cock-a-doodle-doooo!

(All the others hold their ears and turn toward the **ROOSTER.***)*

ALL. *(in unison, to the* **ROOSTER***)* Stop that!!!

ROOSTER. What? What did I do?

PEGGY. You nearly broke my eardrums. No more crowing until sunrise tomorrow.

HENRY. And, hopefully, not even then.

GRETCHEN. Ralph, actually, your crowing hurts our ears.

HENRIETTA. Because you crow wrong.

ROOSTER. Wrong? I crow wrong? How can a rooster crow wrong? I was born crowing. It's what I do. It's my whole career.

GRETCHEN. You crow like this. *(She crows terribly off-pitch.)* Cock-a-doodle-doooo!

HENRIETTA. When you should crow like this. *(Her crows become chicken cackles.)*

DOG. Not like that. Like this. *(His crows become dog howls.)*

CAT. No. Like this. *(Her crows become cat screeches.)*

BYRON. Like this. *(He crows.)*

MELISSA. No, no. Like this. *(She crows.)*

(Now they are all crowing and making horrible sounds. **OINKIE** *appears at the door down left. She sees the others. But then she hears them.)*

OINKIE. *(She covers her ears and dashes across the room and off up right.)* Wee, wee, wee, weeee!

PEGGY. *(to the others)* Wait. What was that?

HENRY. What was what?

PEGGY. Didn't something just flash across the room and run into Oinkie's room?

PIGTAIL. Crying "wee, wee, wee" all the way.

PIGSTY. That was Oinkie.

PEGGY. Henry? You get Oinkie. Pigtail, Pigsty, come with me. *(They exit into the kitchen.)*

HENRY. *(He crosses to the door up right and opens it.)* Oinkie, come on out here. We have a surprise for you.

OINKIE. *(She appears at the door.)* I can't, daddy.

HENRY. Why not?

OINKIE. Because all that crowing makes my teeth rattle.

HENRY. Mine, too.

OINKIE. Some were saying, "Cock-a-doodle-doooo!" Others were yelling "Cock-a-doodle-doo." And a few were crying, "Cock-a-doodle-doooo!" *(She does each of the "Cock-a-doodle-doos" a different way, each more harsh and off-pitch than the others.)*

ROOSTER. Stop, stop! Now you're hurting *my* ears!

GRETCHEN. *(to the **ROOSTER**)* That's how we feel when you're crowing.

ROOSTER. Well, sorry.

HENRIETTA. Starting at dawn tomorrow, Gretchen and I will be giving you crowing lessons.

ROOSTER. Crowing lessons?

HENRIETTA. Until you learn to do it right.

ROOSTER. How embarrassing.

OINKIE. *(She looks at the decorations.)* Decorations!

GRETCHEN. *(to **OINKIE**)* Ours are the best.

HENRIETTA. By far.

OINKIE. *(to **ROOSTER**)* But I thought you were going to bring the moon.

ROOSTER. The moon? Oh, yeah, well, the moon. Well, we tried.

GRETCHEN. But we couldn't quite reach it.

OINKIE. Not even with the ladder?

HENRIETTA. It was higher in the sky than we thought.

ROOSTER. Sorry.

OINKIE. Well, that's okay. The decorations look good anyway.

GRETCHEN/HENRIETTA. We think so.

> (**PEGGY** *enters from the kitchen carrying a big birthday cake with six candles on it.* **PIGTAIL** *and* **PIGSTY** *are on either side of her carrying a cupcake each with one candle in each.*)

PEGGY. Oinkie? Look what we have for you! *(She holds up the cake.)*

OINKIE. *(When she sees it, her eyes grow large. She is very excited.)* A cake? A *big* cake!

PIGTAIL. A big birthday cake!

PIGSTY. Better get a piece of it right now – before Pigtail eats it all up. *(He reaches for a piece.)*

PEGGY. *(She slaps his hand away.)* This cake is for Oinkie. Your cake is in your hand.

PIGTAIL. What? She gets a huge cake like that, and we get these itty-bitty things?

PEGGY. You've been eating all morning.

PIGTAIL. I still have room in my tummy for cake.

PEGGY. *(She chants. NOTE: the traditional song "Happy Birthday to You" is copyrighted and may not be used in performance without the payment of royalties.)* Happy, happy birthday, little Oinkie;
Happy, happy birthday, little piggy;
We've gone to this little fuss…because we're glad you're one of us;
Happy, happy birthday, Oinkie.

ALL. *(Some chant off-key and behind or ahead of the others.)*
Happy, happy birthday, little Oinkie;
Happy, happy birthday, little piggy;

We've gone to this little fuss…because we're glad
you're one of us;
Happy, happy birthday, little Oinkie!

(They cheer with their specific animal sounds, including
ROOSTER'*s still off-pitch "Cock-a-doodle-doo."*)

OINKIE. Oh, Momma! *(She hugs her.)* Pops. *(She hugs* **HENRY**.*)*
Pigtail *(She hugs her and then turns away.)*

PIGSTY. Hey. What about me?

OINKIE. You're so dirty!

PIGSTY. So are you.

OINKIE. *(She looks at herself.)* Oh, well, I wallowed in the
mud down by the creek. Oh, okay. *(She hugs* **PIGSTY**.*)*

PIGSTY. *(He pulls away.)* Ewww! Hugging is one thing. But
hugging girls is yucky!

(The two **HENS** *unfold some big letters suspended from a*
string that say, "Happy Birthday.")

GRETCHEN/HENRIETTA. Happy birthday, Oinkie!

OINKIE. *(She hugs them both.)* Oh, thank you; thank you. *(She*
hugs everyone present with a "Thank you" after each hug.)
I'm so happy, I've totally forgotten about the turtle
bite and the thorns.

PEGGY. The what?

OINKIE. Oh, it's nothing. *(pause)* I thought you had forgotten about my birthday. I thought everybody had
forgotten.

PEGGY. Time to blow out your candles. Come on. Make a
wish.

OINKIE. *(She closes her eyes.)* Mmmm. *(pause)* Okay. I did it.

HENRY. Blow them out. All of them in one blow.

(She does. Everyone claps and cheers.)

PIGSTY. Here, Oinkie. Have some of my cupcake. *(He*
smashes it into **OINKIE**'*s face and laughs.)*

OINKIE. *(She licks it off her lips.)* Mmm-mmm, good! *(She takes*
PIGTAIL'*s cupcake and smashes into* **PIGSTY**'*s face.)*

PIGSTY. *(He laughs and wipes part of it with his finger and then licks the finger.)* It's not good. It's delicious!

PEGGY. Celebration now; food later!

OINKIE. *(She says this in glee.)* Wee, wee, wee, weeee!

> *(There is another cheer as music is heard. They march around the room and stop in frozen positions. The music fades away. The lights fade out on the room, but remain bright on the bed.)*

Scene Seven

(The bed; immediately following)

(AT RISE: **MOMMY** *leads* **RACHEL** *from the up right door to the bed, where they both sit.)*

MOMMY. And that's the story of "This Little Piggy...."

RACHEL. *(She claps.)* That was a good story, Mommy. I liked it. I liked Oinkie the best – because she was sad at first, and then she was happy.

MOMMY. She thought her mom and dad had forgotten her birthday.

RACHEL. But they didn't.

MOMMY. No. That's something parents would never forget, Rachel. Because their children are precious to them.

RACHEL. I know. *(She looks around.)* Where's Daddy? Isn't he going to kiss me goodnight?

MOMMY. Well, he's at the grocery store. He should be home any minute now.

RACHEL. But he doesn't buy groceries. You buy all the groceries.

MOMMY. I told you that tomorrow is a special day.

RACHEL. But you didn't tell me why.

MOMMY. Okay, okay. He's buying things for a birthday party. For a real birthday party. Do you know who's having a birthday tomorrow?

RACHEL. I hope it's not you – because you're way too old already.

MOMMY. *(She laughs.)* No, it's not me. It's you, Rachel.

RACHEL. *(thrilled)* Me?!

MOMMY. Yes. You'll be this many years old. *(She holds up six fingers.)*

RACHEL. Six? I'll be six years old?

MOMMY. That's right. Six years.

RACHEL. Oh, Mommy! That's the same as Oinkie!

MOMMY. That's right. Good for you.

RACHEL. Can she come? Can Oinkie come to my party?

MOMMY. Well, honey, Oinkie doesn't really exist.

RACHEL. She does, she does.

MOMMY. She was just part of my story.

RACHEL. No. She's real. I know she is. I saw her. I saw her.

MOMMY. You imagined that you saw her

RACHEL. Well, then, I'll imagine that I see her again.

MOMMY. Honey....

RACHEL. Like this. *(She squeezes her eyes shut and gives a long grunt.)* Unnnnnhhhh!

MOMMY. You don't have to grunt so hard to use your imagination.

RACHEL. *(with her eyes still closed)* I see her, Mommy. I see her!

(The Lights fade upon the full stage, and the earlier music plays softly. **OINKIE** *dances.)*

RACHEL. And the others, too. I see Mommy and Daddy Pig.

*(***PEGGY*** *and* ***HENRY*** *join* ***OINKIE*** *in the dance. As* ***RACHEL*** *says the following names, they dance too. The music grows in volume, though it should not drown out the spoken lines.)*

RACHEL. And there's Pigtail. She's eating again. And Pigsty. He still hasn't taken a bath. And the Hens and the Rooster, and Joansie and Melissa and Byron. And there's the Dog and the Cat!

(As before, the ***CAT*** *snarls and chases a loose piece of paper that trails behind the* ***DOG***.*)*

RACHEL. *(If* **OTHER ANIMALS** *are used, include this sentence. If not, skip it.)* And all the others. *(Keep these sentences either way.)* I see them Mommy. I see them all.

*(***RACHEL*** *opens her eyes, leaps off the bed, and joins the dancing. She takes* ***OINKIE***'s *hand, and they prance about the room together.)*

ALL. *(Except* **MOMMY**. *They chant as before.)* Happy, happy birthday, little Rachel;

Happy, happy birthday, little girlie;

We've gone to this little fuss...because we're glad you're one of us;

(Even **MOMMY** *enters the dance and chants here.)*

Happy, happy birthday, Rachel!

(They chant and dance or prance even louder as they repeat the song.)

Happy, happy birthday, little Oinkie;

Happy, happy birthday, little Rachel;

We've gone to this little fuss...because we're glad you're one of us;

Happy, happy birthday, Oinkie...and Rachel!

(Several throw confetti as they all cheer and applaud **RACHEL** *and* **OINKIE**, *who raise their hands in victory.)*

(The lights fade to black.)

(The curtain falls.)

PROPERTIES

Scene One

> On the set:
>
> > On the bed: a towel, a large blanket, 2 pillows
> >
> > Table or hat rack near down left door: Peggy's purse (containing a wallet, credit cards, bottle of mouth wash, very long grocery list [use a roll of adding machine paper], a shawl, a tote bag)
>
> **MOMMY:** an apron, a spoon, a pot, three lists of chores
>
> **RACHEL:** toothbrush
>
> **PEGGY:** an apron identical to Mommy's
>
> **HENRY:** mop, water pail, broom, dust cloth, spray cleaner, and misc. other cleaning supplies
>
> **PIGTAIL:** roast beef sandwich
>
> **PIGSTY:** 2 slices of bread
>
> **OINKIE:** teddy bear

Scene Two

> On set:
>
> > Shovel, broom
> >
> > Table or hat rack near down left door: Same as Scene One
>
> **PIGTAIL:** bowl of pig slop, doll with detachable head
>
> **PIGSTY:** half-eaten apple, toy, banana
>
> **OINKIE:** teddy bear

Scene Three

> **HENS:** An A-frame stepladder
>
> **OINKIE:** teddy bear
>
> **JOANSIE:** a large bag of flour (the flour is not seen)
>
> **MELISSA:** a large bag of corn (the corn is not seen)
>
> **BYRON:** a large bag of beans (the beans are not seen)
>
> **DOG:** an armload or bag of birthday decorations, including a 3" wide roll of crepe paper

Scene Four

> **HENRY:** a frilly apron, a mop and pail
>
> **PIGTAIL:** a sandwich, an empty bowl
>
> **PIGSTY:** a bottle of catsup
>
> **ROOSTER:** the A-frame ladder
>
> **GRETCHEN:** a big bandage
>
> **HENRIETTA:** her wing in a sling
>
> **DOG:** decorations from the previous scene, plus the roll of crepe paper
>
> **JOANSIE:** a loaf of bread on a plate
>
> **MELISSA:** corn on the cob on a plate
>
> **BYRON:** one bowl of lima beans, one bowl of pinto beans
>
> **PEGGY:** an apron

Scene Five
>   **OINKIE:** thorns stuck in his clothing

Scene Six
>   **PEGGY:** birthday cake with six lit candles
>   **PIGTAIL:** a cupcake
>   **PIGSTY:** a cupcake
>   **HENS:** large letters on a string or rope that, when extended, spells "Happy Birthday"
>   Several characters to be selected: confetti

COSTUMES

The costumes may be a s simple or as elaborate as desired. The following are suggestions:

MOMMY: a house dress or slacks and blouse, an apron
RACHEL: a nightgown or pajamas
PIGS: pig ears and snouts, regular human clothes appropriate for each character; or full costumes representing pig bodies with perhaps tops such as vests, jackets, or shirts
ROOSTER: beak, rooster comb, webbed sleeves; or full costume representing a rooster
HENS: beaks, webbed sleeves; or full costume representing hens
CHILDREN: clothing appropriate for young farm children
DOG: dog ears and snout, regular human clothes; or full costume representing a dog
CAT: cat ears and snout, regular human clothes; or full costume representing a cat
OTHER FARM ANIMALS AS DESIRED: the basic characteristics of each similar to those described for the animals above; or full costumes representing each animal.

SETTING

The setting may be as simple or elaborate as desired. The following are suggestions:

At stage right (the audience's left) is a small bed, initially for Rachel, and later for Henry. An exit at up right (away from the audience) leads to the bedroom of Pigtail and Oinkie, and an exit at down right (closer to the audience) leads to Pigsty's room. At stage left (the audience's right) is a small dining table with chairs or benches. An exit at up left leads to the kitchen, while the one down left leads outside. The area downstage (or in front of the curtain if one is used) has no furniture and represents several locales. Walls may surround the interior of the house, or stage curtains may substitute for them.